TILLY'S PONY TAILS

Neptune

the heroic horse

TILLY'S PONY TAILS

Neptune
the heroic horse

PIPPA FUNNELL

Illustrated by Jennifer Miles

Orion
Children's Books

First published in Great Britain in 2010
by Orion Children's Books
a division of the Orion Publishing Group Ltd
Orion House
5 Upper St Martin's Lane
London WC2H 9EA
An Hachette UK Company

1 3 5 7 9 8 6 4 2

The Orion Publishing Group's policy is to use papers that are natural,
renewable and recyclable products and made from wood grown in
sustainable forests. The logging and manufacturing processes are
expected to conform to the environmental regulations of the country
of origin.

A catalogue record for this book is available from the British Library.

ISBN 978 1 4440 0082 5

Printed and bound in the UK by CPI Mackays, Chatham, ME5 8TD

www.orionbooks.co.uk
www.tillysponytails.co.uk

For Becky Coffey

One

The start of the school summer holidays
always made Tilly Redbrow happy.
She couldn't wait to have six weeks of
uninterrupted time at Silver Shoe Farm.
She planned to be there every morning,
afternoon and evening. For a pony-mad girl
like her it was going to be great!

Silver Shoe Farm was very special to
Tilly. Not only was her dream horse, Magic
Spirit, stabled there, but it was where she
hung out with her friends, Mia and Cally,

and had riding lessons with the farm's owner, Angela.

Tilly and Magic Spirit had come a long way since they'd joined the Silver Shoe gang. When Tilly looked back she could hardly remember how neglected and nervous Magic had been when he'd first arrived. Thanks to everyone's care and attention, he was now a picture of health. Tilly's dream had come true too. Once she'd only ever fantasised about the horses from her books and magazines, now she was a keen rider with a talent for understanding them. She listened and looked and learned everything she could from other riders, particularly talented ones like Angela, her teacher, and Duncan, the head boy at Silver Shoe Farm. And Brook,

of course, her new-found horse-crazy
brother.

Magic Spirit would always be important
to Tilly. They had an incredible bond.
For other riders Magic could lack
confidence and be very tricky. He played
up for Duncan and made it hard for
Angela to catch him. But with Tilly, he
always behaved. When she rode him, he
responded to everything. It was as if they
were destined to be together. Whenever
Tilly was with him, the trust in Magic's
eyes was clear. When she wasn't there,
Duncan often said that Magic seemed
to have a wild look about
him.

Tilly was riding
Magic regularly now, as
she'd grown out of Rosie,
the pony she shared with
Mia. She still loved Rosie
dearly and saw her every
day, but Mia was also
getting too tall to ride

her, and the girls' parents had discussed finding a new owner for Rosie soon. Tilly dreaded the idea that the little pony might have to leave Silver Shoe.

One balmy summer Saturday, Tilly was working Magic in the sand school. She'd just started doing some jumping training with him, and she'd been having trouble because he was jumping to the left over fences. With Duncan's help, she was trying to teach Magic to keep to the middle of the fences. They had set up a low upright with two poles placed in an upside-down V shape. The poles rested on the top bar like an arrow pointer, helping Magic to keep straight.

'Nice work,' said Duncan. 'It's really helping him. It's important to sort this out now, before he gets into the habit of jumping left. If we don't, the problem will

be exaggerated the more we ask him to
do, and this way, when we build in more
complex jumps and cross-country training,
he'll have a solid base to work from.'

Tilly agreed. She didn't mind
concentrating on the attention to detail
because a horse like Magic deserved
the best quality training, and she was
determined to take him to the top.

'It's great that you'll be around for the
whole summer,' Duncan added. 'With you

on board, Magic's bound to make progress.
Hopefully, he'll be ready to jump some
solid cross-country fences by September.
Right, that's enough for today.'

Tilly pulled up at the fence where
Duncan was leaning. She hopped off Magic
and gave him a rewarding cuddle.

'I'll be here every day,' she said.
'There's nowhere I'd rather be than Silver
Shoe Farm.'

Just then, Tilly's mobile buzzed. She
pulled it out of the pocket of her navy
jodhpurs. There was a message
from Brook:

HEY! SORRY IT'S SHORT NOTICE BUT FANCY
JOINING ME AND MY FAMILY
ON HOLS IN CORNWALL?
NEXT WEEK. WLD
BE GREAT IF U
CLD MAKE IT.
MY MUM WILL
SPEAK 2 UR
MUM. BROOK X

'Well, almost nowhere,' said Tilly. 'Oh dear. Brook's just invited me to go on holiday with him. I'd LOVE to but . . .'

'Sounds too good to miss,' said Duncan. 'Don't worry. Magic will cope. Go and enjoy yourself. I expect you and your brother have lots of catching up to do.'

Tilly smiled. She and Brook definitely had lots of catching up to do. They'd first met on a visit to Cavendish Hall, the exclusive boarding school that Brook, and Tilly's friend Cally, attended. It had been obvious then that there was a connection between them. Now they knew why. Thanks to their matching horsehair bracelets they had discovered they were brother and sister, separated when they were tiny and adopted by different families.

Going on holiday with Brook was perhaps one of the few things Tilly would sacrifice a week with Magic Spirit for. She

looked into Magic's eyes. She knew he'd understand, although the thought of being apart from him made her feel sad.

'It'll only be for a little while, boy. I'll miss you. Maybe one day, I'll take you on holiday with me.'

An image popped into Tilly's head, of her and Magic galloping along a beautiful sandy beach, seawater spraying in their faces. It was wonderful.

Two

Tilly's parents were happy for Tilly to go on holiday with the Ashton-Smiths. Mr Redbrow, being a teacher, said it was 'more educational' to go on the odd family away day to a museum or a castle, rather than spend a week lazing around in the sunshine. Tilly and Adam had been slightly alarmed by this suggestion, but Tilly didn't really mind. She knew her parents had already spent quite a bit of money on her riding lessons, and besides, one week away

from Magic and Silver Shoe Farm was
definitely enough!

Tilly and the Ashton-Smiths arrived
in the Cornish fishing village of Tregenny
on a Sunday afternoon, after a long and
tiring drive. Brook's family had managed
to squeeze Tilly into the back of their
car along with the vast amounts of clutter
they'd brought with them.

As Tilly climbed out of the car over the
various bags and cases, she breathed in the
sea air. It was fresh and breezy. She knew
she was going to have a good time. She
was looking forward to spending more time
with Brook, and his parents had always
seemed like lots of fun when she'd met
them before. They reminded her of her
own family, the Redbrows, but a bit posher
and more chaotic.

The Ashton-Smiths' holiday home,
Avalon Cottage, overlooked a white sandy
cove. Turquoise waves lapped against the
shore and seagulls swooped and squawked
above their heads.

16

Brook helped his
parents unload the
car while Tilly watched
over Doug, the family's
Irish wolfhound. Doug was
very gentle, even though he was almost
as big as some of the ponies at Silver
Shoe Farm. Tilly started to wonder what
everyone at the farm was up to. She knew
Magic Spirit would be well looked after by
Duncan, Angela and Mia but she couldn't
help missing him, just a little bit. It helped
to know that he'd be missing her too.

She hoped they'd get the chance
to do some
horse riding
in Cornwall.
She'd already
spotted

a sign for the Tregenny Farm Stables. She couldn't wait to see what it was like. Just then, a cry from Mrs Ashton-Smith brought Tilly back to reality.

'Oh dear! I've spilled safety pins all over the car boot.'

'Safety pins? What on earth did you bring safety pins for?' said Mr Ashton-Smith.

'Well, you never know when you might need one.'

Brook grinned at Tilly.

'Let's go inside, shall we? I'll show you round.'

The cottage was every bit as lovely as Tilly imagined it would be. Brook led Tilly up a spiral staircase to what was going to be her room. It was very sweet with a blue-and-white striped bedspread and curtains, and a mirror surrounded by seashells. On the wall was a painting of three stallions galloping through the waves. Looking at it made Tilly's spine tingle.

'If you think that's good,' said Brook, noticing Tilly admiring the painting, 'take a look at this . . .'

He pointed out of the window. Tilly stared. She could just about make out the outline of several horses down at the cove, being walked along the sand. She pressed her nose to the glass for a closer look.

'Ah, how perfect!' she sighed.

'They come from the stables at Tregenny Farm. We can visit if you like.

We've been going there for years – every time we've been down to the cottage. We're good friends with the owner, Lillian. We'll have to introduce you, Tilly. And, of course, we'll have to have a ride on the beach. It's a great feeling, taking the horses into the sea – they really love it.'

'I bet,' said Tilly, mesmerised.

That evening, after everything had been unpacked and they'd eaten some tasty Cornish pasties, Tilly and Brook took Doug for a walk. Neither of them had planned it, but somehow they both knew the walk would end up at the Tregenny Farm stables.

'Maybe we're psychic,' Tilly said jokingly, after Brook suggested the detour. 'I was thinking the same.'

'Or we're just horse-obsessed,' he replied, with a smile.

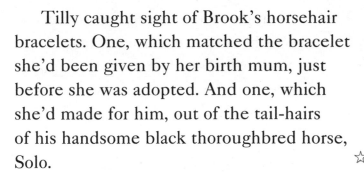

Tilly caught sight of Brook's horsehair bracelets. One, which matched the bracelet she'd been given by her birth mum, just before she was adopted. And one, which she'd made for him, out of the tail-hairs of his handsome black thoroughbred horse, Solo.

Tilly had made lots of horsehair bracelets for her friends, using the tail-hairs of horses that were significant to them. Duncan had Red Admiral's, Cally had Rosie's, and Angela had Pride and Joy's. Tilly liked to think of them as lucky charms. She'd certainly had a lot of luck with hers.

As they ambled down the lane towards the farm, the scent of sea air was replaced by the familiar smell of horse manure and hay dust. Then they heard the sound of hooves clip-clopping on the road.

'I love that sound,' said Tilly.

'Me too,' said Brook.

They turned through a set of cobble-stone gate posts, into the yard. It was much smaller than the one at Silver Shoe, but it looked really pretty with hanging baskets of pink and purple flowers and traditional wooden stable blocks. There was room for about twenty horses. As Tilly and Brook

walked past, the horses bobbed their heads over the stable doors. One of them was a grey, with colouring similar to Magic's, only a little paler. Tilly stopped to say hello and her thoughts instantly went to Magic. How was he getting on without her? She hoped he wasn't playing up.

'Come and meet Lillian,' said Brook, leading her by the elbow.

Lillian was standing by a water trough, talking to some holiday makers. She was small and plump, with grey hair and a friendly face. As soon as she saw Brook she excused herself, turned towards him and threw her arms out.

'Brook! Haven't you grown? Mind you, I say that every year. And this must be Tilly. Your mum told me everything. Brother and sister, eh? How marvellous! Welcome to Tregenny Farm, Tilly. Are you keen on horses?'

Before Tilly could reply Brook gave a chuckle.

'That's an understatement! Actually, Tilly's got an amazing way with them. She sort of speaks their language. She helped me and Solo when he was spooked by a water jump. And she rides a beautiful grey called Magic Spirit, who doesn't like working with anyone but her.'

Tilly blushed.

'An instinct for horsemanship then,' said Lillian, smiling. 'Maybe it's got something to do with those bracelets you wear. Your mum told me you've both had them since birth. Anyway, you're welcome to have a ride with the Tregenny Farm horses any time. They love new faces, wha with all the tourists around. And it's always a treat for them to be ridden by people who actually know about horses – not like *those* poor chaps . . .'

Lillian nodded towards the people she'd been talking to, a girl and her parents. The parents were gazing around interestedly, but the girl was clearly anxious. She flinched whenever there was a whinny or snort. Tilly could tell that this was her first experience of a stable yard.

'They're trying to arrange a trek,' whispered Lillian. 'The parents are keen for their daughter to join in, but something tells me she's going to back out before she's even mounted. She seems to think horses have fangs and eat humans! We introduced her to our gentlest, dearest old thing, Seaweed, and she nearly jumped out of her skin!'

Tilly gave a puzzled smile. She knew it was important to have a healthy respect for horses but she couldn't understand why anyone would be frightened of them.

Three

Next morning, Tilly woke to the sound
of seagulls squawking. She lay in bed for
a while, staring up at the painting of the
three stallions. She
imagined one of
them was Magic.
Perhaps the other two
were members of his family.
Like Tilly and Brook, maybe they'd been
reunited and, at last, were able to gallop
along the beach together.

Tilly wondered if Magic had long-lost siblings. After all, when she'd found him by the roadside in North Cosford, he'd been alone. No one knew anything about his background or breeding. She twiddled her horsehair bracelets, especially the one made from Magic's tail, and thought about going back to see the horses at Tregenny Farm. She couldn't wait to go for a ride.

Eventually the peace was disturbed by the sound of pots and pans being clunked in the kitchen. The aroma of frying bacon drifted up the stairs.

'Come and get it when you want it!' Tilly heard Mrs Ashton-Smith call.

She stumbled out of bed and down to breakfast.

'The weather forecast is for sunshine,' said Mrs Ashton-Smith, as Tilly came through the kitchen door. 'Let's take advantage of it and go down to the cove for the day. We can take a picnic with us.'

'Sounds perfect,' said Tilly, between mouthfuls of her bacon sandwich.

It took a while for them to gather their things. There were several panics about missing picnic blankets and punctured lilos, and Mr Ashton-Smith decided he couldn't bear to be without his mobile phone, in case he needed internet help with a tricky crossword clue.

By the time everyone was ready, Tilly and Brook were bursting to get to the beach. They ran the entire way, pretending to race each other, although neither of them cared who won – they were just happy spending time together.

They staked out a section of sand with windbreaks and parasols. Mr Ashton-Smith unpacked the games bag, which contained a cricket bat, Frisbee, tennis racquets, and skittles, plus several buckets and spades. They looked fun, but the thing Tilly most wanted to do was go and say hello to the little group of ponies who were at the far end of the beach, busily giving seaside rides.

Brook caught her looking at them.

'They're the ones from Tregenny Farm
we spotted from your window yesterday,'
he said. 'They're here every day. We'll go
over after lunch, when it's quieter. What
about a dip in the sea? Last one in is a
loser . . .'

Rising to the challenge, Tilly pulled
off her denim shorts and ran to the water's

edge. The cold spray prickled her skin, making her squeal and retreat. Brook, however, wasn't deterred. He crashed through the waves, then dived and came up. A clump of seaweed was stuck to his forehead. Tilly whooped with laughter.

'Come on, sissy! Get in! It's lovely once you're used to it!'

'Yeah, right!'

'Look, *she's* not bothered by a bit of cold water,' said Brook, pointing to a girl, about Tilly's age, floating in a rubber dinghy.

Tilly recognised the girl from yesterday evening. It was the same one who'd been scared of the Tregenny Farm ponies. She seemed happy enough in the sea, splashing around and humming to herself.

'Odd, isn't it?' said Tilly, as she and Brook trod water. 'That some people find horses frightening. I mean, I know it's important to be careful around them, but they're not monsters.'

'It's easy for us to think that,' said Brook, 'because we've had lots of good experiences with them. We're not frightened because we understand and know what to expect. Other people don't get that opportunity. They're scared of what they don't know.'

'I hope that girl gets a good experience at Tregenny Farm. So she stops being frightened . . .'

Suddenly there was a flurry of splashing. Legs and arms thrashed in and out of the water. An unexpectedly big wave had knocked the girl out of her dinghy. She managed to get hold of it again, but she was gasping for air.

'Are you okay?' asked Brook.

'Yes,' the girl replied, smiling. 'I'm always falling out. It's fun. Don't worry. I'm a strong swimmer. I swim for my county.'

'Even so, you need to be careful,' said Brook. 'The waves can get quite big here.

They come up unexpectedly. And the currents are strong. It's not like swimming in a pool.'

'Okay,' said the girl, but it was clear she hadn't really taken him seriously. She looked at Tilly.

'I like your plaits,' she said. 'You look like Pocahontas.'

'Uh, right, thanks,' said Tilly. 'My name's Tilly, short for Tiger Lily. And this is my brother, Brook. What's your name?'

'Megan.'

'Nice to meet you, Megan. We saw you at Tregenny Farm yesterday. Are you planning a trek?'

'Not if I can help it,' said Megan. 'My parents want me to. My mum liked riding horses when she was a girl, so she thinks I should like it too. But I'll stick with swimming – it's safer.'

'Maybe you should give it a try,' said Tilly. 'You never know.'

'We're both keen riders,' said Brook. 'There are some lovely horses at Tregenny

Farm. Honestly, you shouldn't be frightened.'

'They don't look lovely to me. They're so big! And jumpy! And they bite!'

'Not if they're well trained,' protested Tilly.

Brook could see they weren't going to change Megan's mind.

'Are you on holiday?' he asked, changing the subject.

'Yes. We're staying at the big guest house on the seafront.'

'Megan!' came another voice. It was Megan's father. He was wading into the water towards them. 'Megan! Time to go!'

'Not now, Dad,' said Megan glumly.

'Yes, now,' he said. 'Mum's waiting for you. We're going to see the horses on the beach . . .'

'*Noooo!*' said Megan.

Tilly and Brook looked at each other and shrugged.

As they watched Megan trail reluctantly behind her parents, Tilly wished she could

make Megan see horses differently. If only
she'd give them a chance, she'd find out
just how wonderful they really were.

Four

After a delicious picnic of saffron buns,
cheese, and strawberries,
Tilly and Brook, still
thinking about Megan
          and her fear of
              horses, took
                 a walk
                 along the shore to see the
                 ponies. To them, it was a
                 treat, so it seemed strange
that Megan found it so awful.

37

As they approached, they could see a track marked out in the sand. It was being manned by two girls from the stables, who were both wearing matching navy jodhpurs and white t-shirts with 'Tregenny Farm Rides' written on them. They looked like experienced riders, and reminded Tilly a bit of Mia and Cally.

'Hi, Rachel. Hi, Sally,' said Brook, stopping to chat.

'Oh, hi, Brook. Lillian said she saw you yesterday. How are you? Down for the summer hols?'

'Yep. Just for a week. This is my sister, Tilly.'

He put his arm around Tilly's shoulder. It felt very strange hearing him describe her as his sister. Strange but good.

'We didn't know you had a sister,' said Rachel.

'Nor did we,' said Tilly.

'It's a long story,' said Brook, at the same time.

Then they looked at each other and

grinned.

The girls introduced the three ponies.
There was a small, friendly chestnut
called Coral; a bay with a white blaze and
stockings called Smuggler; and a large
skewbald called Neptune. As Tilly stroked
and greeted each of the ponies, she found
herself drawn, in particular, to Neptune.
There was something about the kind
expression in his eyes. He had a wise look,
as though he'd been around for a while,
and had learned everything he needed to
know.

Like other horses Tilly had formed
friendships with, Neptune was immediately
interested in her horsehair bracelets. He
sniffed around them with great fascination.

'What are you after, eh?' said Tilly
affectionately. Neptune gazed at her, as
though he was trying to figure her out, then
carried on sniffing.

'He's the biggest of the bunch – 15hh,'
said Sally. 'We let him take older riders
up and down the shoreline. He's really

good natured. He's done a lot of RDA –
that's riding with the disabled – so he's
always careful and gets good results from
whoever's riding him.'

'He's lovely,' said Tilly, stroking his
neck. 'He seems so gentle and kind.'

'Do you guys want a ride?' asked
Rachel. 'It's pretty quiet at the moment.
Coral gets restless if she's standing about
too long.'

'That would be great,' said Brook.
'Come on, Tilly. I'll introduce you to beach
trekking. You take Coral and I'll take
Neptune.'

Tilly glanced at Neptune. He was the
horse she most wanted to ride. She couldn't
explain why. It was an instinct. But it made
sense for Brook to ride him, since he was the
tallest. If Brook had to ride one of the other
smaller ponies it would look pretty silly!

Rachel and Sally gave them riding hats
and also gave them each a leg up. Neptune
marched forward on Brook's command.
Coral fussed for a minute, but when she

saw what Neptune was doing, she followed.
Perhaps she sensed in him what Tilly did,
that he was strong and dependable, the
sort of character people looked up to. No
wonder he made a good RDA horse.

'Let's go along to those rocks and back,'
said Brook, pointing to a rocky outcrop at
the opposite end of the cove.

They trotted along the sand, not far from the water. It was lovely to have the waves beside them and a clear blue sky above. They were followed by a group of children, who chattered and giggled behind them. Even Megan, who was sitting with her parents, licking an ice-cream, gave them a wave.

'Hi, Megan.' Tilly waved back. 'Come and say hello?'

But despite her parents' encouragement, Megan shook her head nervously, and Tilly decided to leave her to it.

When they reached the rock-pools they paused.

'How does it feel riding Neptune?' Tilly asked eagerly.

'Great. He hasn't got the athletic feel I'm used to with Solo, but he's very responsive. He seems to consider every movement he makes, which gives a really steady ride. There's nothing excitable or skittish about him. How's Coral?'

'A bit fussy,' said Tilly, stroking Coral's neck – she didn't want to offend her. 'But she's sweet. She only wants to go where Neptune goes.'

'He's quite heroic-looking. Maybe she fancies him?'

Brook and Tilly laughed. Neptune shook his head. Then Coral did too.

'Now she's copying him!'

On the way back, where the beach was quiet, they had a light canter at the edge of the water. Neptune and Coral seemed to love it. The salty spray and the lap of the waves didn't bother them at all, in fact it seemed to encourage them.

Tilly loved it too, although at one point, when Coral stumbled, Tilly realised she hadn't been paying enough attention and nearly lost her balance. Her foot came out of the stirrup and she wobbled to one side. Luckily, she managed to right herself and was very glad she did – she'd already had one swim that day!

'Did you see what happened back there?' said Brook, as they returned the horses to Rachel and Sally. 'When you lost your stirrup, Neptune looked round to check you were okay. It looks like he already feels a bond with you. At one point I thought he was going to try nudging you back on with his nose.'

'What a clever boy!' said Tilly, impressed. She patted his shoulder and let him nibble at her bracelets. 'I'll have to make sure I have a ride with you this week.'

'Any time,' said Sally.
'And you're welcome to
help out around the stables
if you're missing some
pony action,' added
Rachel. 'I hate
being away from
my horses – even
if it's just for the
weekend.'

Tilly and Brook
both smiled. That was something they
could definitely relate to.

Five

Later, back at the cottage, Tilly washed,
dried and plaited her hair – a process which
always took ages, especially when her
mum wasn't around to lend an extra pair
of hands. When she had finished it was
time to join Brook and his family for a
cup of tea in the garden. Before she went
downstairs, though, she texted Mia. After
her ride with Neptune and Coral, Magic
was on her mind.

HEY MIA. WHAT'S HAPPENING AT SS? IS MAGIC MISSING ME? X

Mia texted back immediately.

ALL GOOD. HOW'S UR HOLIDAY? M XXX

Tilly replied.

GR8T! FOUND SOME HORSES!
BUT TELL ME MORE ABOUT MAGIC AND SS!!! X

Even though Tilly was enjoying her break, she was desperate to catch up on all the Silver Shoe news. And although she had Neptune and the other Tregenny Farm ponies to get to know, nothing could beat Silver Shoe Farm and her favourite horses there. This time, Mia sent a more detailed reply.

EVERYTHING COOL. ANGELA AGREED ROSIE CAN STAY AT SILVER
SHOE AS A RIDING SCHOOL PONY. HOORAY! LUCKY CHANCE CHEWED
JACK FISHER'S NEW RIDING JACKET. AND YES, MAGIC IS MISSING U.
COME HOME SOON! X

Tilly laughed. It was great news that
Rosie was going to stay at Silver Shoe.
Tilly, Mia and Cally had all learned to ride
on her. She was a strawberry roan with a
charmingly sweet nature and long, pretty
eyelashes. Now, other girls and boys would
be able to enjoy riding her too.

Tilly was secretly pleased that Magic
was missing her. She didn't like the idea
of him being unhappy, but it reassured her
to know he was thinking of her as much
as she was thinking of him. It also meant,
when her lovely holiday with Brook was
over, she had something to look forward to:
her reunion with Magic.

'Tilly! Tea's ready. There's scones
and jam and clotted cream if you're
hungry . . .'

Mrs Ashton-Smith's voice sailed up the
stairs. Mmm. At the thought of the scones,
Tilly's mouth began to water. Spending
all day on the beach was hungry work.
She straightened her horsehair bracelets,
smoothed her plaits and ran downstairs.

It was warm in the garden, although
the sun was slowly making its way
towards the horizon. They sat on a little

patio, surrounded by bright flowers and
butterflies. Brook poured tea into cups
from a china pot. It all felt very grown-
up and civilised. If
this was a Redbrow
family holiday,
thought Tilly, she
and Adam would
be arguing over a
computer game or
something silly but,
in a way, she enjoyed
that.

'It's so nice
to have you two
together for a
whole week,' said
Mrs Ashton-Smith.
'Sometimes I catch a
glimpse of you both,
and I can't believe
you were ever
separated. There are
so many similarities

between you. The eyes. The dark hair. The smile. Even some of your mannerisms are the same.'

'It's quite uncanny,' said Mr Ashton-Smith, as he sipped his tea. 'Now that you've found each other, do you want to know more about your birth mum?'

Tilly and Brook looked at each other and smiled.

'It would be amazing to know where she grew up and what she did. Of course, we already know she was horse-mad,' said Brook.

'The horse in the photographs,' added Tilly. 'It would be great if we could find out more about that horse as well. Maybe it's where our horsehair bracelets came from.'

52

'Yes, there must be something significant about those bracelets,' said Mr Ashton-Smith.

'Maybe they're the key to finding out more?' suggested Mrs Ashton-Smith.

Tilly stared into the distance. It would be fascinating to know. Maybe it would explain how her affinity with horses had come about. Ever since she was little, she'd loved them. It was instinctive. She'd never been frightened, like Megan. It was hard to imagine what that was like. She'd always felt safe and content in their presence.

From the patio, she could see across the treetops, right down to the cove and the entrance to Tregenny Farm. She had such a strong feeling that horses were her life. There was nothing she liked more than looking after them, riding them, training them. Maybe Brook was having the same thought because he looked at her and said,

'Perhaps we should see if we can squeeze in an early evening ride? What do

you think? Work off some of this clotted cream before dinner . . .'

'Good plan,' said Tilly eagerly. But she wasn't bothered about the clotted cream. She just wanted the ride!

Six

'Why don't you take Neptune this time?' said Brook. 'I can see you're dying to have a ride on him.'

Tilly was delighted. And Lillian, the owner of Tregenny Farm, was more than happy to let her and Brook take the horses for a quiet evening ride along the beach.

'Neptune's been restless all afternoon so I'm sure he'll appreciate it,' she said. 'And Merman loves a splash in the sea. That's if you can get him to leave his

hay-net – that horse just loves eating, and he can be rather lazy.'

Merman was going to be Brook's ride, and Brook was determined to use his strong legs to get Merman going more forward.

He and Tilly borrowed riding boots and hats.

'Can we give them a groom before we take them out?' asked Tilly. 'I've really missed just brushing and pampering the horses since we've been away.'

'Of course,' said Lillian. 'I'm sure they'll enjoy the extra attention.'

They tied Neptune and Merman beside each other and  wiped them over with a stable rubber.

'Your coat is so shiny,' she said, as she ran the rubber across Neptune's hindquarters. 'It's one of the shiniest I've ever seen.'

Lillian overheard and explained. 'It's all that salt water. It's a great natural conditioner. It's also fantastic for their legs, and it's been known to really speed up the healing of injuries too.'

Tilly wiped Neptune's eyes and nose with a sponge and brushed out his mane. As she combed his tail she couldn't resist collecting the loose hairs. They were brown and white, because he was a skewbald, and she hadn't made a bracelet out of two different colours yet. She didn't know who she'd give it to, she just felt compelled to make it.

'I'm really looking forward to going out on you, Neptune,' she said, folding the tail-hairs into her pocket.

Neptune stared at her with his kind, inquisitive eyes.

'I hope it will be a ride to remember.'

When they were ready, they led the

horses to the mounting blocks and climbed
on. Tilly immediately sensed Neptune's
calm, steady manner. He stood perfectly
still as she swung her leg over and adjusted
her position. It was as if he wanted to make
the task easier for her.

Merman didn't make things quite so
simple for Brook. As soon as Brook was
in the saddle, Merman turned to face the
opposite direction, then wouldn't budge.
Brook spoke firmly and asked with his leg.

Lillian hadn't been joking when she'd
said Merman didn't like to leave his hay-
net. Not only that, but it was a struggle
getting him to leave the yard. He put his
ears back stubbornly, ignoring Brook's
commands.

'He's been a bit naughty recently,
taking advantage of the less experienced
riders,' said Lillian apologetically, as she
approached a rather disgruntled-looking
Merman.

'Come on, Brook, let's see you work
your magic,' said Tilly, giggling.

'Fancy a swap?' Brook replied. 'You're the magic girl with Magic Spirit after all!'

'I'll stick with Neptune, thanks.'

Brook wrapped his legs around Merman and gave him a good couple of hard kicks with his heel, to which Merman reacted at once, following Tilly and Neptune begrudgingly out of the yard.

They managed to get as far as the entrance to the beach path but, true to his reputation, Merman found every opportunity to ignore instructions.

'Don't wait for us,' said Brook. 'We'll be here forever by the look of things. Go ahead and we'll meet you on the beach.'

'Okay. See you in five . . . or ten?'

'Twenty more like!'

Tilly laughed then nudged her heel and asked Neptune to walk forward. He obliged and soon they were trotting down the sandy path towards the cove.

After a little while, Tilly could see the end of the path ahead of them. The pine

trees opened onto a clear view of sand, sea
and sky. The sky itself had a beautiful soft,
pinky colour, which reflected on the water
and made everything glow. It was serene
and magical.

'Ah,' sighed Tilly. 'How lucky you are,
Neptune, to get to ride here all the time.
Maybe one day Brook and I will move to
the seaside and run our own stables. I'm

sure Magic Spirit and Solo would enjoy the
beach. They're our horses back in North
Cosford. They're clever and gentle, just
like you. You'd like them, I know you
would.'

Neptune nodded his head as though he
was agreeing with her. Tilly could sense
the connection between them growing
stronger with every step. He responded

to each tiny little adjustment she made. There was no impatience or unexpected movement. She felt completely safe in his care, as if she'd been riding him for years.

'I can picture it all,' she continued. 'A little cobble-stone farm, just like Tregenny, with room for fifty horses and ponies, plenty of pasture, and training facilities. We could breed and train event horses. And, of course, we'd take in horses that have been abandoned or injured. It'll be perfect.'

At the edge of the path, Tilly decided to wait for Brook. She was keen to tell him her plans for the beach-side stables. She drew Neptune to a halt, leaned forward and stroked his shoulder. She could feel the silky smoothness of his coat and the warmth of his body, but suddenly there was something else as well; a tension, a twitch.

'What is it, boy? What's got you so alert?'

Neptune pricked his ears and stood to attention. At this, Tilly *knew* there was

something going on. She tried to reassure
him by patting his neck. She reminded
him to wait for Merman and Brook, but
there was something distracting him.
He wanted to obey Tilly's request to
wait, but at the same time, he wanted to
walk on.

In the end, the 'something' won and
Neptune walked forward onto the beach.

'Whoa there!' called Tilly, trying every
aid she could to get him to stop. But just
as she thought he was responding, his pace
actually picked up. He wasn't moving in a
wild or out-of-control way. He was steady
and measured, but determined. Before
Tilly knew it they were cantering along
the sand.

She realised that in order to maintain
her own balance, she had to keep her
cool. She went with the motion and
hoped Neptune would run himself out
after a short while. Nevertheless it was
quite frightening. Just then, she spotted
something in the sea ahead of her.

At first it looked like a seal, then she saw it was a person. A girl, in fact.

'Help! Help me!'

It was Megan. She was splashing and panicking.

Tilly's heart raced. She looked around for Brook, but he and Merman still hadn't reached the beach. There was no time to wait for him. Neptune slowed as he got to the water's edge, but Tilly understood his intention. Momentarily, he nodded at the sea, as if to say 'shall we go for it?'.

Without hesitating, Tilly nudged him forward and they crashed into the water. The cold was shocking but it didn't matter. Tilly knew they had to get to Megan before it was too late.

'Help!' she cried.

Neptune moved in the water with ease and grace. Tilly didn't need to give him any further instruction. He seemed to know instinctively what he had to do. He waded towards the girl, holding his head above the water.

The waves didn't make it easy. Occasionally they were big enough to reach Tilly's waist. Each time they broke, they drenched her with freezing spray. But this was no time to worry about keeping dry.

In the deeper water, Tilly made sure her feet were secure in the stirrups. She sat low and close to Neptune's neck, to help her balance, and when she was near enough she reached for Megan's hand.

'Hold on!'

Megan's cold, clammy fingers gripped her wrist. By now, she was whimpering with fear. Tilly remembered she was frightened of horses and tried to reassure her.

'Don't be scared,' she said. 'Neptune's here to help you. Let me pull you towards him. We'll get you out of the water.'

Then she leaned forward and whispered to Neptune, asking him to stand strong and stay very calm, so that Megan wasn't startled. Neptune immediately responded. He stood perfectly still against the swell. Tilly dragged Megan towards her and hoisted her up into the saddle. She fixed her

hands to the reins and held them in place.
Slowly Neptune the heroic horse heaved
himself around and carried them to the
safety of the shore.

Seven

By the time they were out of the sea, and
had managed to dismount, Brook and
Merman were heading towards them. As
soon as Brook realised Tilly had been in
the water, he quickened his pace.

'Tilly! Are you okay?'

'I-I'm fine,' she said. 'It's Megan.'

She put her arm around the girl, who
was shivering and sobbing.

'We found her in the water,' Tilly
explained. 'She was struggling to stay up

. . . calling for help. Neptune just . . . went for it.'

As she said this, the enormity of what had just happened dawned on her. She and Neptune had rescued Megan from drowning. There had been no hesitation. No uncertainty. Without panic or confusion, or any thought for their own safety, they'd gone straight to her aid and got her safely out of the water.

And here they were, safe on the sand.

Suddenly she felt amazed by it all.

Neptune stood back, calm and quiet. He kept himself a little distance from them, as though he was giving them space to recover. Tilly wondered if he'd really listened to her advice. It was clear he didn't want to give Megan any more shock than she'd already had.

He waited peacefully, as if nothing out of the ordinary had happened. He looked around, occasionally shuffled his feet, and sniffed the ground. Tilly could see he was the kind of character who didn't let things go to his head, which made her admire him even more.

She dreaded to think what would have happened if she and Neptune hadn't arrived when they did, or Neptune hadn't been the kind of horse he was. And it was lucky they understood each other so well. They'd trusted one another. They'd believed in each other's instincts. Tilly was overwhelmed with an urge to give Neptune a hug.

'I'm so proud of you. That was the bravest thing I've ever seen a horse do. You're a true hero!'

Neptune pricked his ears. Tilly looked over to where Brook was asking Megan if she was okay. Megan was almost too upset to speak. Her body trembled and shook with every sob. Tilly left Neptune and went over to them.

'What were you doing alone in the water?' Brook asked. 'I warned you about the current.'

'I-I-I . . . wanted . . . just . . . an evening swim . . . my parents were hassling me about riding . . . I wanted to escape . . . it looked so flat . . . so calm . . . I didn't mean to . . .'

'Don't worry. You're safe now,' said Tilly. 'Everything's going to be fine.'

'We'll call the coastguard,' said Brook. 'They'll probably send a rescue team to check on you. And we should call your parents. It could have been a very bad situation. Look at you both. You're shivering.'

He took off his jumper and wrapped it round Megan's shoulders, then he took off his t-shirt and gave that to Tilly. The t-shirt wasn't very warm, but at least it was something dry. With all the drama, Tilly had barely noticed that she was soaked from head to toe.

Ten minutes later the beach was swarming with people. The rescue team arrived with stretchers and silver blankets. They checked Tilly and Megan over and concluded that Megan was in shock, but otherwise fine.

'That's some horse you've got there,' said one of the rescue workers.

'He's not mine,' said Tilly. 'He lives at Tregenny Farm. His name's Neptune. He knows this beach really well, so I guess you could say he's a local hero.'

'He is indeed. Maybe we could recruit him for the coastguard team! We've had a few dogs helping patrol the beaches before but never a horse.'

Tilly smiled. It seemed like a perfect idea.

Brook's parents came down with a thermos of hot chocolate. They'd seen the drama unfold from up on their patio, so it was a big relief to find everyone safe and sound.

'I don't think my heart's ever thumped so fast,' said Mrs Ashton-Smith. 'I could see the girl swimming. I could see the horse running into the water. I knew one of you would be on it, but I couldn't work out which of you it was. Then I saw those plaits swinging about. It was terrifying!'

'I'm sorry if I frightened you, Mrs Ashton-Smith,' said Tilly.

'Oh, don't be sorry,' she replied. 'You've saved someone's life.'

The next people to arrive were Megan's parents. They ran down the beach. Behind them were more people from the nearby guesthouses, who were concerned about what was going on.

Megan's mum burst into tears and her dad had a tight, stricken look on his face.

'We told you not to go down to the beach alone! We told you the current was too strong!' he cried.

'You were supposed to be in the guesthouse garden,' said Megan's mum.

They sounded angry, but Tilly could tell they were just upset. When they reached their daughter they threw their arms around her and hugged her as though they would never let her go. Suddenly, Tilly wished she had her mum and dad to hug *her*. It was all too much. She was shaken and tired. Her eyes filled with tears.

'We'll call your parents when we get back to the cottage,' said Mrs Ashton-Smith, putting her arm around Tilly.

'They'll be really proud. You've been so brave. And Neptune has been too. Why don't you go and say well done to him.'

Tilly nodded. Another cuddle with Neptune would be the next best thing to a cuddle with her mum and dad, or even Magic Spirit.

She went over to Neptune and together they found some peace and quiet, away from the fuss and commotion.

'Hey, boy,' she whispered, stroking his nose. 'I know you're not one for showing off, but you might find you're a bit popular in this town for a while . . . don't let it go to your head.'

She looked into his eyes and smiled. In that instant she felt really close to him. It seemed as if there was no one else around but them. It was a feeling she'd had before, with Magic Spirit, with Samson the show-jumper, with all of her special horses.

She thought of the tail-hairs she'd collected from Neptune earlier and knew exactly what she'd do with them.

Neptune lowered his head and allowed her to scratch his ears.

'You're so gentle,' she said. 'Strong and brave, but gentle. You're the kind of horse that no one needs to be frightened of.'

Eight

Tilly's mum and dad were impressed but understandably worried when they heard the news. She spoke to them on the phone for over half an hour and next morning they kept sending text messages saying things like:

TIGER LIL. JUST CHECKING UR OKAY? LOVE DAD. XXX

Tilly replied to every single one because she knew they'd only worry

otherwise. She also texted Mia and Cally. She didn't want to brag so she didn't mention the rescue in too much detail, but she couldn't wait to tell them all about Neptune.

HEY GUYS. I'VE MET THE MOST AMAZING HORSE. WE HAD A BIG ADVENTURE TOGETHER YESTERDAY. TELL U WHEN I GET BACK. BIG KISSES TO MAGIC. XXX

At breakfast it was all anyone could talk about.

'I expect it'll make the local news,' said Mr Ashton-Smith, between mouthfuls of scrambled egg. 'You might even make the front page!'

'Those poor parents. They must feel so guilty. Very irresponsible though. Imagine. Why would anyone allow a young girl to go swimming on a quiet beach, all by herself?' said Mrs Ashton-Smith.

'They didn't *allow* her. That's the point,' said Brook. 'Megan sneaked down to the sea without telling them. She told us she's a good swimmer and swims for her county. I warned her about the strong current but I guess she wasn't paying attention.'

'Ironic, isn't it?' said Mr Ashton-Smith thoughtfully. 'Megan's afraid of horses and then a horse goes and saves her.'

'I wonder if the experience will help her get over her fear.'

'I hope so,' said Tilly, thinking how wonderful that would be.

Suddenly the telephone rang. Mr Ashton-Smith got up to answer it, while the rest of them tucked into more toast and scrambled eggs. A few minutes later he returned to the table.

'Ahem. That was Lillian from Tregenny Farm. She's got reporters coming to the stables this morning. They want to do a piece on the heroic horse and his rider. Are you up for a bit of media stardom, Tilly?'

Tilly smiled and blushed. 'Can I wash my hair first?'

By the time they got to Tregenny Farm, there were reporters already talking to Lillian and some of the stable girls. When Tilly walked through the gate they stopped and applauded her. She felt like a superstar. It was nice, but she wanted to make sure they understood the true hero was Neptune.

'Watch out for daft questions, Tilly,' said Brook, with a nudge. 'I sometimes get reporters wanting to ask me about my competitions. The ones who know about horses are great, but there are a few who don't get it at all.'

'I'll be careful,' said Tilly. But before she could prepare herself, she was swamped by the eager gang.

'Hello, Tilly. I'm from *The Cornish Chronicle*,' said a glamorous lady with red lipstick. 'Well done on your dramatic sea

rescue. When did you notice the girl? Did you think about your actions or did instinct take over?'

'Er, it was Neptune who noticed. And he had the urge to go in and rescue her. I just went along with it.'

'Do you think he was very brave?' said another reporter.

'He was just doing what his instincts told him. He's a very special horse, with an amazing personality. He's used to working with disabled people.'

Tilly was pleased with that answer.

'It must take a skilled rider to handle a horse in that situation. Are you a skilled rider, Tilly?' said the red lipstick lady.

'Um, I practise a lot. And I sort of know how to get on with horses.'

'Really?' said one of the reporters. 'Like a modern day Doctor Doolittle?'

The others laughed. Tilly felt quite embarrassed. She fingered her horsehair bracelets nervously. Luckily Brook stepped in, cool and calm.

'My sister has an amazing way with horses. It's a talent she was born with.'

Tilly glanced at Brook. 'Thanks,' she mouthed.

'Can we get a photo? Of you and the horse?' said one of the photographers.

'I don't see why not,' said Lillian, as she ushered Tilly away from the crowd.

Neptune was standing outside his stable. Sally, who Tilly recognised from the beach, had just finished grooming him. When he saw Tilly he pricked his ears.

'Good morning,' said Tilly, patting his neck. 'How does it feel to be a local hero?'

Neptune shook his nose, as if to say it was no big deal.

'You're so modest,' Tilly whispered, kissing him on the nose.

'Do you think he'll be okay with the cameras?' asked one of the photographers.

'He'll be fine,' said Sally. 'Nothing fazes Neptune.'

Indeed, as the cameras clicked and flashed, Neptune was calm and unruffled. Tilly was the one who got nervous. She adjusted her plaits then adjusted them again. She tried to smile but the corners of her mouth kept twitching.

'Relax,' whispered Brook. 'Imagine you've just won the Badminton Horse Trials.'

With this in mind, Tilly's confidence grew. She tried different poses, with and without a riding hat and gloves. She smiled for some pictures and looked serious for others. By the end, she felt so grand it was as if she really *had* won Badminton.

Nine

The Ashton-Smiths were leaving early next morning 'to beat the traffic', Mr Ashton-Smith explained. Although Tilly was excited about seeing her family again, and returning to Silver Shoe Farm and Magic Spirit, she was sad to be leaving Cornwall and Tregenny Farm after everything that had happened.

She folded her clothes into her suitcase.
They mainly consisted of different
coloured polo shirts, jeans and jodhpurs,
with the odd pair of shorts and swimwear
for the beach. Other than that it was stable-
suitable clothing all the way, which was all
she had in her wardrobe.

'What about a nice dress? Or a pretty
blouse?' her mum sometimes said.

'Is it practical for mucking out in?' Tilly
would reply with a smile.

When their suitcases were packed,

it was time
for Tilly and
Brook to make
a special trip to
the newsagents
in the village.
They were
hoping to see
the story about

Tilly and Neptune before they left.

'Do you think there'll be a colour
photo?'

'Of course there will. You'll have to add it to the collage on your wall, or frame it and put it up in the Silver Shoe club room.'

'Definitely. Although I hope it doesn't make Magic jealous . . .'

They pushed through the door of Robinson's Local Stores. A little bell rang as it opened. Inside, the shop was very old-fashioned. It was like stepping back in time. Tilly gazed around. There were jars of old-style sweets on the shelves and everything looked as though it had been there for decades.

'Good morning, Mrs Robinson,' said Brook.

The shop keeper, a friendly-looking elderly lady in a lime green cardigan, looked up and smiled.

'Ooh. Is this her?' she said, coming closer to Tilly and putting her glasses on.

Tilly resisted an embarrassed giggle.

'Michael!' the lady called into the back room, with a thick Cornish accent. 'The pony girl is here!'

She turned back to Tilly.

'It's an honour to meet you, young lady. You're famous now, you know.'

Michael appeared clutching a copy of *The Cornish Chronicle*. He passed it to Tilly. The headline on the front page read: *Mysterious Pony Girl Saves Drowning Child*.

Beneath it was a picture of her and Neptune standing outside the stable block. Neptune looked very regal and proud. Tilly looked as though she was trying to fight off more giggles.

'I must say, that photo doesn't make you *look* very mysterious,' said Michael, in a polite but puzzled manner.

Tilly laughed.

'I'm not. I just love working with horses,' she replied.

Brook glanced at her and caught her eye. They both knew there was more to it than that, but it wasn't something they could easily explain.

They bought five copies of *The Cornish Chronicle* and were given one copy free by the Robinsons. Tilly wondered if that might be too many, but then it wasn't every day she made headline news.

'Enjoy your celebrity status, mysterious pony girl,' Brook said jokingly, as they wandered back up the cliff road.

'We should take a copy of the paper to show Neptune. And then I guess we'll have to say goodbye to him.'

'Er, hang on a minute. There's something I need to do quickly. I won't be long,' said Tilly. 'I'll meet you at the entrance to Tregenny Farm in ten.'

Brook nodded and went ahead. Tilly stood back and stared at the row of seafront guest houses. She wanted to work out which one was Megan's. *The biggest one*, she remembered her saying. Tilly stared up at the building and wondered how she would find them. She hoped they hadn't left already. There was no sign of anyone.

Moments later, one of the front doors flung open. Megan and her mum came out. They ran towards Tilly and showered her with hugs and kisses. It was quite overwhelming.

'We saw you from the window. We can't thank you enough for what you did,' said Megan's mum, as though she couldn't get the words out fast enough.

'I hardly did anything, honestly,' said Tilly. 'It's Neptune you need to thank. He's the true hero. I tell you what . . .'

Tilly had an idea.

'I'm on my way to Tregenny Farm now. Why don't you come with me? You can thank him yourselves.'

Megan's expression was a mixture of fear and curiosity.

'I know you're a bit scared of horses,' said Tilly. 'But I want to show you there's

nothing to be afraid of, now you know what wonderful, heroic things they can do.'

Megan nodded. Tilly could see the hope start to shine in her eyes. She was glad.

'Can we go with her, Mum? Can we go and see Neptune?'

'Okay. For a short while.'

Together they walked the last stretch of the cliff road down towards Tregenny Farm. Brook was waiting on the corner, and when he saw Megan and her mum he gave Tilly a knowing smile.

Neptune was in the yard.

'Let's go and say hello,' said Tilly. 'Come with me. We'll do it together.'

She took Megan's arm and led her towards him. Neptune remained calm and still, but as they drew near, he lifted his head and turned to look at them. It was a friendly look, but Tilly could feel Megan's grip on her arm tighten.

'It's okay,' whispered Tilly. 'He's only showing an interest. I think he recognises you.'

Keeping hold of Megan, she slowly took her hand and placed it on Neptune's shoulder. Gradually, Megan began to relax.

'He's so warm and silky,' she said.

'He's enjoying it,' said Tilly, watching as Neptune gently curved his neck towards Megan and gave her a little sniff.

'You can give him one of his treats if you like,' said Sally, the stable girl, coming over to them. 'He loves carrots.'

She took a carrot from her pocket and passed it to Megan. Tilly showed her how

to offer it to him on the flat of her hand.
Megan giggled and squirmed as his tongue
licked her, but she didn't seem frightened
any more. Tilly was delighted. It was great
to see Megan's confidence grow. She felt
proud that she and Neptune had helped
make it happen. They were a good team.

'Before you go,' said Tilly. 'I wanted to
give you this.'

She reached into her pocket and
pulled out the horsehair bracelet made
from Neptune's tail-hairs. Megan stared,
wide-eyed, as Tilly tied it round her wrist.

'Wear it always. It will remind you of
Neptune and how he rescued you. It might
even bring you good luck.'

'Thank you.'

'And one more thing,' said Tilly,
smiling. 'Promise me you'll learn to ride
one day.'

'I will,' said Megan, grinning.

Tilly wasn't sure whether this would
really happen, but as Megan and her mum
walked away she heard Megan say, 'Mum,

when we get home, maybe we could look into those riding lessons you keep talking about. It doesn't seem half so scary now!'

Ten

Early next morning, before breakfast, Tilly couldn't resist saying another goodbye to Neptune. While everyone was busy getting showered and washed, she left a note on the kitchen table then ran down to Tregenny Farm.

The sun had just risen and apart from the occasional seagull cry, there was a wonderful quietness in the air. Tilly loved this time of day.

Getting up early to muck out and feed at Silver Shoe Farm never bothered her. She looked forward to early starts, because it meant peaceful time alone with the horses.

As she turned into the yard, Tilly realised she wasn't the only one who liked to be up and about at the stables. Lillian was there too, wearing a huge woolly cardigan, cradling a mug of tea, checking on all of the horses. She had lots of energy. Tilly imagined Angela might be like her when she was older.

'Good morning, Tilly.'

'Morning, Lillian. I've come to say goodbye to Neptune. We're going home today.'

'Oh, shame. Neptune will miss you.'

'I'll miss him too. I hope I'll come back again with Brook's family, but for now our holiday's over. It's time for me to get back to Magic Spirit and Silver Shoe Farm.'

'Yes, Brook told me about that. Sounds like you've got a real gift with horses. Neptune obviously thinks so.'

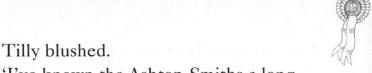

Tilly blushed.

'I've known the Ashton-Smiths a long time. Brook's been coming here since he was a little boy. It was obvious from the beginning he had a knack with horses. It's amazing to think you've got it too, even though you didn't grow up together. Uncanny. There must be something in your background.'

'Yes,' said Tilly. 'We'd like to find out more about our birth mum, who gave us the horsehair bracelets, but we don't really know where to start looking,'

'Well, it may be a long shot, but I've heard about a tribe of Native Americans who used to wear bracelets made from the tails of their horses, a bit like yours. It was on a radio programme a while ago. That's all I can remember I'm afraid. But maybe it's worth looking into.'

Tilly thought for a moment and nodded.

'Thanks. I'll look it up.'

'Anyway, I'd best get on,' said Lillian.

'Spend all the time you want with Neptune. I'll see you soon, I hope.'

'Bye.'

Tilly went over to Neptune's stable. He was inside, enjoying his morning feed. When she peered over the door, he chomped for a bit then came towards her.

'I've come to say goodbye. I'm going to miss you, boy.'

She ran her hand down the smooth part of his nose and tickled behind his ears.

'Keep up the good work. The beaches will be safer with you around!'

Neptune nodded. Tilly took one last look at him then turned away. She felt sad about leaving him. It was like saying goodbye to a close friend. Even though she'd only known Neptune a short while, she knew there was a natural connection between them. She could feel it. She couldn't explain it, but she definitely knew it was there.

As she walked back to the cottage, taking one solemn step after another, she reminded herself that Magic Spirit was waiting for her. Just a four-hour car ride to go and she'd be back in North Cosford with him, which was a thought that cheered her up enormously.

Unfortunately, the journey took ages, because the traffic was heavy. So it was no surprise that the first thing Tilly wanted to do after being dropped off by the Ashton-Smiths was visit Silver Shoe Farm. By now, she was itching to see Magic and the other horses.

'We'll all go,' said Mr Redbrow, realising it was the only way he'd get to spend time with his daughter.

On the way Tilly showed them a copy of *The Cornish Chronicle*.

'We're very proud of you,' said her mum. 'Everyone's been talking about it.'

'That horse should wear a superhero cape,' said Adam. 'They could make a comic book about him: *Neptune to the Rescue!*'

Suddenly, Tilly was distracted. She felt a tingle up her spine as the car made its way through the tunnel of silver birches. She saw the fields stretching ahead and the white buildings in the distance, which meant the turning to Silver Shoe Farm was just around the corner.

As soon as Mr Redbrow pulled the car into the lane, Tilly climbed out and sprinted up to the five-bar gate. She pulled it open and took a deep breath of happiness as she saw Magic in the yard being shod by the farrier. She couldn't get to him fast enough and when he saw her approach, he quivered with joy. He pricked his ears and began pulling towards her, nearly taking the farrier with him.

'Oh, Magic! I've missed you! Hello, gorgeous boy,' she said, as she showered him with kisses and cuddles.

Instantly she was lost in the reunion. She barely noticed Angela, Duncan, Mia and Jack Fisher as they gathered round. They were all keen to hear about Tilly's 'big adventure', but they knew better than to get between her and Magic.

'That horse *adores* her,' said Jack Fisher. 'In all my years of equestrianism I've never seen anything quite like it.'

'He's been restless and impatient the whole time she's been away,' said Duncan. 'Now she's back with him, you watch, he'll be as good as gold.'

'At least he's got taste,' said Tilly's dad proudly.

Tilly just stared into Magic's eyes, amazed she'd managed to be apart from him for a whole week. And in that instant she realised, although there'd be other horses in her life from time to time, like

Neptune, the one that really mattered, the
number one dream horse, was standing
right in front of her. It couldn't be better.

Pippa's Top Tips

In order to give your horse the best quality training, it's important to pay attention to every little detail.

Your horse or pony will need shoeing every four to six weeks, depending on the amount of roadwork they have been doing. Keep a close eye for any risen clenches (nails) or loose shoes that might need attention.

Remember, hooves will need regular trimming, even if your horse or pony doesn't have shoes on.

Always keep your hand flat when offering a horse or pony a treat.

If your horse is lazy and reluctant to leave home, you'll need to use plenty of leg. Try a good few kicks with your heel, or you might even need to tickle him up with a whip if he ignores your leg.

Salt water is a great natural conditioner – it's fantastic for horses' legs, and it's also been known to speed up the healing of injuries.

No matter what distractions there might be when riding, always keep your concentration, because a simple trip or a stumble can easily throw you off balance.

Riding is all about confidence, so don't run before you can walk. In other words, don't be tempted to do more than what you and your pony feel capable of.

Always try to be smart and tidy when you're riding – it gives a much better impression.

Likewise, a well-groomed pony with a tidy mane and tail, with whiskers and feathers (fetlock hair) trimmed, also creates a much more professional picture.

including pony tips, quizzes and everything
you ever wanted to know about horses –
visit www.tillysponytails.co.uk